Striker Jones and the Midnight Archer

Striker Jones and the Midnight Archer

By Maggie M. Larche

ISBN 978-1484016909

Bulk order discounts are available for schools, fundraisers, community groups, and other functions. Please see www.elementaryecon.com for more information.

Publisher's Cataloging-In-Publication Data
(Prepared by The Donohue Group, Inc.)

Larche, Maggie M.
Striker Jones and the Midnight Archer / by Maggie M. Larche.

p. : ill. ; cm. -- ([Striker Jones ; 2])

Summary: Striker Jones and his friends solve a new batch of mysteries while away at summer camp. Each mystery teaches a new economic concept.
Interest age level: 008-012.
ISBN: 978-1-4840-1690-9

1. Economics--Juvenile fiction. 2. Economics--Fiction. 3. Mystery and detective stories. I. Title.

PZ7.L27 Stm 2013
[Fic]

Contents

Chapter 1

Pop Secret

"Let's do this!" said Bill Flannagan. "Six weeks of swimming, sports, canoes, campfires, and no parents!"

Striker Jones laughed with his best friend. The two boys were in line with 20 other kids in the school parking lot, waiting to load a bus that would take them to Camp Leopold for part of the summer. There they would join up with kids from across the county.

This was Striker's first year to attend the camp, but Bill had attended five years in a row.

"You're gonna love it," said Bill.

"I'm just glad I get to go," said Striker, thinking back to his mother's goodbye that morning. She hadn't exactly cried, but Striker had noticed some definite sniffling. Now, he kept glancing over his shoulder, expecting to spot his mom hiding in the azalea bushes or on the school roof, simply to sneak a few more looks before he left for camp.

"Look, there's Amy and Sheila," said Bill, pointing to their two friends, Amy Beckham and Sheila Meyers. Striker and Bill had known Sheila for years, and Striker had had a crush on her for almost as long. Amy moved to their school the previous year, and the four friends had been inseparable since.

The two girls were getting out of a car driven by Sheila's dad. He jumped out of the car and lifted Sheila high into the air in a big hug.

"Dad!" Striker heard Sheila say with a red face. "I'm too old for this!"

"Bill! Striker!" yelled Amy. She waved the one hand that wasn't loaded down with her canvas bag and pillow.

"Hey!" called Striker and Bill.

Amy ran over, while Sheila gently disengaged herself from her dad's arms. Striker watched as she kissed her dad quickly on the cheek and ran to follow Amy, waving behind her as she went.

"I'm so excited," Sheila said as she and Amy joined the boys. Her blues eyes sparkled. Like Bill, Sheila had also attended the camp for years.

"Me, too!" said Amy as she quickly pulled her red hair into a ponytail. "I've never been to camp before. This is the first time we've lived in one place long enough for me to go!"

"It's fabulous," said Sheila. "The cabins are so cute, and we get to decorate our bunks however we want."

"And there's every sports competition you can think of," said Bill, "plus a bonfire every night."

"And we get to do adorable crafts," continued Sheila.

"And kayak and canoe and snorkel," said Bill.

"And the lake is just gorgeous," finished Sheila with a sigh.

"Don't forget the best part," added Striker. "No Ralph!"

"Yes!" they all shouted together. They threw high-fives and laughed. They were thrilled for the summer away from the class bully, Ralph Johnson.

"All right, kids," said a counselor at the front of the line. He held a clipboard and pencil. "Time to load up!"

Sheila and Amy squealed and ran to add their luggage to the pile of bags beside the bus. Striker and Bill hoisted their backpacks onto their shoulders. They were off!

The bus ride passed fairly quickly between jokes and choruses of "100 Bottles of Beer on the Wall." The kids never seemed to get past 85 bottles before the song petered out, only to be started anew five minutes later.

Sheila and Amy were sitting in front of Bill and Striker. Both the girls turned backwards in their seats to chat with the boys.

"So, lots of kids come from other schools, right?" said Amy.

Bill nodded. "Yep. Why?"

"I was just thinking, since I don't know any of them, maybe I'll pretend to be someone else for the summer." She turned to Sheila. "Do you think I could pull off a French accent? How's *theez*?"

"Terrible," said Sheila with a laugh.

"Okay. No French. Then maybe I'll be the daughter of a millionaire. Or an orphan!"

Striker laughed. "Try all you want, Amy, but I don't think you could ever pull off being anyone but yourself."

Amy looked at Striker. "You could pretend to be someone else this summer. It must get tiring being 'Striker Jones, Boy Detective.'"

Striker was known for solving mysteries that left others in the dark. He had discovered solutions to many sticky problems in the past and now had a reputation among his classmates as a real detective.

"Don't be silly," Sheila answered for him. "Striker's the best detective around. He shouldn't hide his gift!"

Striker felt red creeping up his neck. Time to change the subject.

"Look," he said. "We're leaving the highway. Are we getting close?"

"No," said Bill, looking out the window, "but we are almost to my favorite part of the bus ride!"

He explained as the bus rumbled around country roads. "There's this lady that sells bags of flavored popcorn by the side of the road. We always stop, and everybody always buys a bag and eats the popcorn on the way to camp. Look! We're here!"

The bus pulled off at a roadside stand.

"Oh, no," said Striker. He patted his pockets as kids jammed the bus aisle. "I didn't realize I'd need money. I didn't bring any."

"No problem," said Bill, sliding out of the seat. "You can share my bag."

They piled off the bus with the other kids and joined the line at the stand.

"One small bag, please," Sheila said to the old woman behind the stand when it was her turn.

"Butter, cheese, caramel, or kettle?" asked the saleswoman, tucking a stray gray hair underneath the bandana she wore on her head.

"Kettle, of course!"

"Me, too!" said Amy.

"Here you go, sweethearts." The woman handed two bags over and smiled.

"Thanks!" The girls gave the lady their money before turning away.

Bill stepped up to the stand.

"I'll take a small cheese, please." He turned to Striker. "Sound okay?" Striker nodded. "I'd get two, but I don't have enough money. There's still a decent amount for us to share though."

"Thanks, buddy!"

Striker and Bill loaded back onto the bus behind Sheila and Amy and headed for their seat. But when they reached their spot, they found something interesting waiting on them.

Sitting on the cracked green vinyl of Striker's seat was a small paper bag filled with popcorn. Striker guessed from its sweet smell that it was the caramel variety.

"What's this?" he asked the girls.

"We don't know," said Amy, opening her bag. "It was there when we got on."

"Did someone misplace it?" asked Sheila.

"Who misplaces a bag of popcorn?" said Bill. "Maybe it's for you, Striker."

Striker gave one last look around the bus and then shrugged his shoulders. "Well, I'm certainly not going to turn it down!"

He picked up the bag and plopped into his seat. Amy and Sheila turned back around and began chatting with one another.

"Who do you think put it there?" asked Bill quietly. "One of the girls?"

"How could they? We were with them when they bought their bags, and they each only got one." He peeked over the seat in front of him. "And they both still have their bags."

Striker glanced around the bus again. Most of the kids were either still in line or standing outside the bus, munching their popcorn. There were only five other campers already back in their seats.

"My guess," he continued, "is that it was one of those two boys." He pointed first ahead a few seats, where one brown-haired boy with glasses tipped his large bag upside-down into his mouth, and then behind him, where a red-haired kid licked cheese powder from his fingers as he held his own large bag.

"Of course," Striker went on, "I don't know either one of them, so I don't know why they'd buy me popcorn. And I don't understand why they would keep it a secret."

"Why those two in particular?" asked Bill. "Every kid on here has a bag of popcorn."

"Yes," said Striker, popping his first fluffy kernel into his mouth and grinning. "But those guys are the only ones that bought the large bag."

Why does that matter?

Solution

The more you spend on something, the more likely you are to spend just a little bit extra on a related purchase.

People do this all the time. When your family is already taking a long vacation, they're more likely to spring for a fancy hotel than they would if they were going on a short trip. Or when you're already paying $10 for a movie ticket, you're more likely to buy a $3 candy bar to go with the show than a 50-cent pack of gum.

So when Striker realized that someone had overheard that he couldn't buy his own popcorn, and then had been nice enough to give him a bag, he guessed that it was someone who probably had already bought a lot of popcorn for himself. That person would be more likely to spring for the extra little bag for Striker than someone who had spent less money in the first place.

* * *

Striker never did find out that it was Charlie Johnson who had secretly given him the popcorn – the red-haired boy who sat a few seats behind them on the bus.

Charlie had had a rough year at school. He'd been the target of the school bully from the first day of class, and he was fed up after months of teasing.

Charlie's cousin Ralph was always tough, and Ralph never got picked on. So Charlie decided to copy him. And when better to try his new macho approach than at summer camp?

Unfortunately for his plan, when Charlie heard that Striker couldn't buy any popcorn, he felt sorry for him. He chose to put off becoming No-More-Mister-Nice-Guy for just a little bit longer in order to help Striker out.

But, Charlie told himself, he would keep his good deed quiet. He couldn't ruin his new "bad boy" image on the very first day! He'd try again to be tough tomorrow.

Chapter 2

Mysterious Roommates

When the buses arrived, counselors stood by as the campers filed off and picked up their luggage. Striker's bus was one of a few filling the dirt road in front of the camp entrance.

"Looks like a lot of kids," he said to Bill.

Bill nodded. "Yep. Even after coming here so long, I've had some years where I didn't know any of the guys in my cabin." He picked up his duffel bag from the pile of unloaded luggage. "But don't worry. You and I should be together. My mom requested it when she registered me."

Sure enough, both Striker and Bill were assigned to Cabin 9.

Each cabin was sparsely furnished, with two sets of bunk beds, one regular twin bed, a linen closet, and five dressers. The clapboard walls were bare.

"Dibs," said Bill, vaulting onto the top bunk of the bunk bed nearest to the door.

"Hi," said a stocky boy with light blond hair. He was leaning back on the lone twin bed reading a comic book, his stuff piled on the floor beside him.

"Hi," said Striker. He placed his backpack on the lower bunk and then introduced himself and Bill.

"Richard Moseby," said the boy, pointing to his chest. "How ya' doing?"

Just then, two more boys entered the cabin: one very short, and one very tall.

"Hey," said the tall one. "I'm Jared Wieczorek." He turned to the boy next to him. "What was your name again?"

"Chris Patinski." Chris kicked his shoes off and jumped onto the remaining lower bunk.

"Hi," said Bill, and the boys introduced themselves.

"Hey, awesome!" said Richard, looking at Jared. "A guitar!"

Striker and Bill exchanged an impressed look.

"Yep." Jared patted the guitar case slung over his back. "Like I could leave it home for all of camp. I need my baby by my side."

"Cool," said Bill.

He turned to Striker, rubbing his hands together. "Well, I guess let's unpack. Then we can go get some grub."

"Sounds like a plan. I'm starved."

Striker quickly pulled his clothes out of his bag and haphazardly threw them into dresser drawers.

Bill turned his own bag upside down over an open dresser drawer and let the clothes tumble in.

He shoved his last pair of socks into the overstuffed drawer so that he could close it. "Done! Now let's eat."

Both Chris and Jared were still unpacking, so Striker turned to Richard. "Want to come?"

"Sure," said Richard. He shut his comic book and jumped up from the bed.

The three boys walked to the dining hall.

"Looks like Amy and Sheila aren't here yet," said Bill, surveying the room.

"That doesn't surprise me," said Striker. "I had the feeling they'd spend more time settling in than us."

"Should this poster go here or here?" asked Bill, cocking his head to the side and squinting. "And what color curtains look good with my eyes?"

Richard and Striker laughed as Bill batted his eyes.

"Are those friends of yours?" asked Richard.

Striker nodded. "We all go to school together."

"Come on," said Bill. "I think I see hot dogs!"

* * *

After a delicious lunch of hotdogs, fries, and fresh peaches the boys walked back to the cabin.

"We should hurry," said Striker, looking up. The sky was rapidly darkening as thunderclouds rolled in.

"Yikes," said Richard. "I hope the storm doesn't cancel tonight's welcome bonfire. It's one of my favorite events."

"Me, too," said Bill. CRACK! An enormous thunderclap suddenly shook the ground. "Uh oh . . ."

The three boys broke into a run as fat drops began falling from the sky.

They burst through their cabin door minutes later, already soaked.

"Let's see if we can find a towel or something," said Striker, shaking the water off his head.

Bill opened the closet door and began pulling out items.

"Sheet, pillowcase, sheet." He yelled to be heard over the noise of the storm. "Hey, what's this?" Bill pulled his head out of the closet and turned to Striker and Richard. He held a crumpled red item.

"It was stuck in the bottom corner," he said, opening it. "Hey, cool shirt!"

"Someone must have left it last summer," said Richard. He grabbed a sheet and toweled himself off. "Geez, listen to that wind!"

Bill held the shirt out at arm's length. "The Philosophy Club," he read. "Huh." He turned the shirt around and continued. "Josh Weaver. Kari Martin. Jared Wieczorek. Chris Patinski."

"Wait a minute," he said. "Jared Wieczorek. Chris Patinski. Aren't those the two guys who are staying with us?"

"Yeah, I think so," said Striker, walking beside Bill. "But I thought they didn't know each other."

The room suddenly flashed white with a lightning strike, throwing the boys' faces into sharp relief.

"Maybe it's a different Jared and Chris," said Richard.

"Wieczorek? Patinski?" said Bill. "They're not exactly common names."

The room shook with a massive thunderclap.

"So they're in a club together," said Striker, taking the shirt to examine it. "That's not a big deal." He paused. "But why pretend they'd never met?"

The three boys stared in silence at the shirt. Rain pounded the roof of the cabin. Richard was the first to speak. "You don't think there's something . . . sneaky going on, do you?"

"What do you mean?" asked Bill.

"Well, I can't think of many reasons why they'd lie about knowing each other. And the ones I can think of seem kind of, well, underhanded."

"Like what?" asked Striker.

"Like," said Richard, "maybe they're planning to cheat in some competition, where they'll make everyone think they've never worked together before, but they've actually been practicing with each other for months."

"And so they'll take everyone by surprise and win!" said Bill. "It could happen."

"Or maybe they're going to run some sort of scam," continued Richard, warming to his subject. "One of them gathers information and passes it back to the other. And no one would suspect them of being in cahoots."

Bill gave a low whistle.

The wind lashed rain against the windows, sounding like several gunshots hitting the glass. All three boys jumped.

"Or," Richard said, lowering his voice to a dark whisper, "maybe they've sworn revenge on someone who's at this camp. And the best way to get that person is to work as a team, but they've got to hide that they're cooperating, so they pretend they don't know each other."

Bill nodded solemnly. "That is usually how it happens in murder mysteries."

The three boys looked at one another with wide eyes.

BAM!

The door to the cabin burst open, just as lightning lit the sky. Two dark figures stood in the opening – one very tall, one very short.

"Ahhhh!" screamed all three boys.

"Whoa!" said Chris, as he and Jared came into the room, dripping with water. "What's up with you guys?"

Striker, Bill, and Richard drew close together and backed away from the doorway as one.

"It's just a thunderstorm," said Jared. He sat on the floor and pulled off his wet sneakers. "We'll probably have lots of them this summer, so you might as well get used to it." He laughed.

Chris emptied his pockets onto his dresser. He threw down some spare change, a couple of guitar picks, and a package of mints.

"It's not the thunderstorm," Richard finally said. He ignored the shushing sounds that Bill was making and squared his shoulders. "It's this." He pulled the red t-shirt out of Striker's hands. "We found this in the closet."

Bill clapped a hand to his forehead. "Now we're done for," he moaned quietly.

Chris and Jared stared at the shirt.

"Darn," said Jared after a moment. "Chris, I knew we should have hid it under the bed."

"So you do know each other?" said Bill, gulping.

"Yep," said Chris. He raised his hands. "You caught us."

Bill threw a worried look at Striker, but Striker wasn't paying attention. He disengaged himself from the huddle with Bill and Richard and walked over to Chris's dresser.

"Why'd you lie?" asked Bill, turning back to Chris. He straightened up and put on a brave face. "You can tell us."

"It's not . . ." Richard leaned forward and whispered, "illegal, is it?"

Striker turned to face the room and laughed. "Bill, Richard. Relax. It's not what we thought."

How do Chris and Jared know each other?

Solution

Chris and Jared are in a band together!

When Chris emptied his pockets, Striker saw that he had been carrying some guitar picks. But Jared was the one with the guitar!

When two items go together, they are called complements. Peanut butter and jelly, a left shoe and a right shoe, a tennis racket and tennis balls – these are all pairs of complements. Having one item allows you to get more use out of the other.

A guitar pick on its own is not much use. It needs to be paired with a guitar in order to fulfill its purpose. A guitar and a pick are complements.

When Striker saw that Chris had an item that Jared would need, and vice versa, he guessed that they were connected through music. He wasn't sure why the two had lied about knowing each other, but it seemed much more likely that it had something to do with a band than with some of the dastardly plots Richard dreamed up.

* * *

"You guys would have found out tonight," said Chris. The boys were standing around the room, drying off with some towels that they had finally found in the closet.

"The Philosophy Club is our band. Me and Jared are the only two members here at camp, but we're still pretty good. We can both play the guitar, and I play harmonica when we perform together. When we got here, a counselor I know from church asked us if we would mind playing at the welcome bonfire tonight. He wanted it to be a surprise for the campers, so we couldn't tell anyone."

"We figured," said Jared, "that rather than lie to you guys about how we knew each other, we'd just pretend we'd never met. We were afraid we'd give it away otherwise."

"Well, I guess we won't hold it against you," said Bill.

"Even if you did almost give us heart attacks," said Striker, laughing.

"I'm just glad you're not really up to some evil plot," said Bill. Striker nodded.

"I don't know if I can forgive so easily," said Richard.

Jared and Chris exchanged uneasy looks. "Look, man," started Jared, "we really are sorry –" but Richard cut him off.

"Nope. Sorry. There's no way I can get past this." He paused, a wide grin spreading across his face. "Unless, of course, you're willing to let me play your guitar."

The guys all laughed.

"Deal."

Chapter 3

Relay Race Riddles

"Morning, boys!"

A few days after camp began, all the girls were gone on a field trip to a nearby Native American reservation while the boys had a field day. The following day, they would switch places.

The owner of Camp Leopold, Mr. Cutchins, was addressing the group of about 40 boys. He was a grey-haired man with glasses and a full beard. "I'm glad to see you men wide awake on this gorgeous morning. We're going to have a fantastic time today. And who better to lead us in all this merriment than the other half of the Leopold dynamic duo – our head counselor, Jamie!" He gestured to his left where Jamie stood with all the other male counselors. "Take it away, Jamie!"

Jamie stepped out from the others. He wore shiny, reflective sunglasses, hiking boots, and a crew cut. "Thanks for the intro, Mr. Cutchins!" He grinned out at the campers. "Today we'll have lots of fun and have a great time getting to know each other better! We'll have several competitions, some serious and some silly. I hope you're all ready to run and maybe even get wet!"

The boys all cheered. It was only midmorning, but the sun was already beating down on them.

"Jamie's my favorite," said Bill to Striker. "He always comes up with the best ideas."

"He rocks," agreed Richard, standing nearby. "Do you remember last year when he helped us build the world's largest ice cream sundae?"

"And then helped us start the world's biggest food fight with it!"

The boys laughed as Jamie began speaking again.

"First thing we're going to do," said Jamie. "Everybody take your shoes and socks off!"

Striker and Bill looked at each other in surprise.

"You heard the man!" said Richard.

All the boys took their shoes off, some sitting on the ground, others kicking their shoes off as they stood.

"Whoops," said Striker as he tilted sideways while pulling off his left sock.

"Okay, guys," said Jamie. "Socks, if you've got 'em, go in your pockets so you don't lose them. As for your shoes – I want you to throw them into a nice big pile here in the middle of the field."

"Why not?" said Striker with a laugh as he set off for the middle of the field.

All the boys jostled one another as they ran together, tossing their shoes into one pile. By the time they were done, there was a mountain of sandals, sneakers, and boots.

"Now let's make it interesting," said Jamie. He walked to the pile and mixed the shoes all together. A mixture of laughter and groans rose from the crowd.

Jamie turned to face the boys again and smiled. "The object is to find your shoes and put them back on as quickly as you can. The first five kids to do so get a swanky camp t-shirt."

Everyone laughed.

"Okay," said Jamie, "make a circle around the shoes. Stand back about 30 feet." He marked it off for the kids.

"On your mark, get set . . . go!"

The boys attacked the mountain.

"Whoa!"

"Found one!"

"Watch it!"

"Mine!"

While Bill zoomed around the pile, Striker ducked to avoid a tennis shoe sailing through the air like a perfectly thrown football. Unfortunately, he wasn't fast enough the second time and couldn't avoid a sneaker thrown directly into his stomach.

"Ooof . . ." he said, doubling over. "Hey," he looked at the shoe, "this is actually mine!"

It took Striker a while to find his second shoe, and he was among the last to finish. As he'd expected, Bill was one of the winners. Richard finished near the end with Striker.

"We'll nail the next one," Richard said, as Bill ran back to them, pulling his new bright blue t-shirt over his head as he went.

"Very nice," said Jamie. "Next up – a water relay race! If you'll all come over this way." He gestured to a row of buckets filled with water. "Let's split up – four kids per team."

The boys began milling around, talking and breaking into teams.

Bill, Striker, and Richard turned to a red-headed boy standing nearby. His arms were crossed, and he was digging his toe into the dirt. Striker recognized him from the bus on the way to camp.

"Teammates?" Striker asked him with a smile.

"Sure!" he said eagerly, uncrossing his arms. "I mean, uh, whatever." He shrugged.

Bill introduced himself, then Striker and Richard. "What's your name?"

"Charlie Johnson." He shifted awkwardly as if unsure of whether to shake hands or not. He finally settled for slouching back onto his heels.

"Johnson?" said Striker after a moment. "We've got a kid named Johnson in our class at school. Ralph Johnson." Striker looked at Charlie more closely. "You actually kind of look like him."

Bill stared at Charlie. "Hey, you're right! You're not related, are you?"

"Yeah, I am. He's my cousin."

Bill and Striker exchanged looks.

"Good to know ya', Charlie," said Richard. He clapped his hands. "Now, let's win!"

Jamie held his hands up to regain everyone's attention. "All right. The object of this relay race is to transfer as much water as possible from your bucket in front of the line to the bucket at the back of the line. You'll be passing these milk jugs from person to person to move the water." He held up a jug with the top cut off to make a bigger opening. "Anybody notice anything unusual about these?" he asked.

"There are holes in the bottom!" yelled someone.

"You've got it," said Jamie laughing. "Each milk jug has lots of little holes punched in the bottom, so the water will be leaking out as you move it from one bucket to the other.

"The team with the most water in their back bucket when time runs out wins."

"Sounds simple enough," said Bill.

Jamie tapped his chin. "Now, I think that's about it . . . Oh wait." A devilish look came into his eye. "There is one thing I forgot to mention. You've got to pass the water jugs over your heads!"

Everyone laughed.

"So I hope you're ready for a shower!" shouted Jamie. "And . . . GO!"

Striker's team jumped into action, scrambling to form a relatively straight line. Charlie, who was first, ran up to the front water bucket and filled the milk jug. He quickly passed it over his head to Bill, who was next in line.

Bill, sputtering as water cascaded down his face, passed the jug to Striker, who sent it on to Richard. By the time Richard had dumped the jug into the back bucket, there was very little water left. Luckily, the four boys were laughing so hard, they didn't especially care.

The same thing was going on across all the teams. Boys hurried to pass the milk jugs back and forth, getting wetter by the minute and falling all over themselves on the slippery grass.

"Yo, Charlie," shouted Richard. "Catch!"

He sent the empty milk jug sailing back to Charlie at the front of the line. Charlie caught it with a surprised and then delighted expression and dashed back to the water bucket to refill.

By the time the relay was over, everyone was soaked. Striker relished the cool, clean feeling of the water on his skin under the warm sunshine. He stretched his arms out and bumped fists with his teammates. They hadn't won the relay, but it had been a good time.

Jamie chuckled as he called the boys back together again.

"Having fun yet?" he asked.

"Yeah!" yelled the kids.

"Good! We've got one more competition coming up before lunch. This one's a little more intense, but I think you guys are up for it."

"Yeah, we are!" shouted Richard. The crowd laughed.

Jamie grinned. "That's the spirit! Now, this is another team challenge. For the sake of simplicity, let's keep the same teams as the water relay race. For this one, you get to practice before the actual race because some of the tasks are a little tricky.

"In this relay race, there are several different activities to go through. Here are the rules.

"First, each team will have to run four laps around the bases." He gestured to the baseball field behind him.

"No prob," said Bill to Striker.

"Next, each team will have to make four shots on the b-ball court over by the lake. No moving on until you've made all four baskets," he said, pointing his finger at the crowd of boys while donning a mock stern expression.

Bill began counting out the rules on his fingers.

"Next," Jamie continued, "you'll have to run the tires on the ground by the courts – back and forth four times.

"And finally, each one of you must swing over the sand traps – otherwise known as the sand volleyball courts – using the ropes that we have hung for that purpose."

Bill looked at his fingers in confusion. "I think I lost track," he said to Striker. "Was that three or four things?"

"Four," said Striker. "I think."

"We'll have to time each team," Jamie was saying, "because there isn't room for everyone to run the race at the same time. Two teams will go at a time. Everyone else can watch and cheer!"

"Whew. That's a bunch to remember," said Richard to his teammates. By the looks on everyone's faces, other teams seemed to be thinking the same thing.

"Now, I know it's a lot," said Jamie, holding up his hands. "Which is why we're giving you one hour to try out the activities and get a feel for the correct order. We've got camp counselors stationed along the way if you need help."

"What's the prize if we win?" one boy yelled from the crowd.

"It's good," said Jamie. "The winning team gets to go into lunch first. You're going to be hungry after this one!"

All the boys cheered before breaking back into their groups. Some headed to the basketball courts or baseball fields.

"Let's get crackin'," said Richard, rubbing his hands together.

"Okay," said Striker. "Should we try basketball first?"

"I'm game," said Bill. The other boys nodded.

On the court, the boys found a free goal and grabbed a ball. They took turns shooting. Richard sunk his first shot immediately, but Striker, Bill, and Charlie all missed.

"That's all right," called Richard as Charlie returned from chasing the ball. "Let's try it again, men!"

Richard made yet another basket, followed by misses from Striker and Charlie. Bill managed to make his shot with a well executed layup.

As they practiced for another ten minutes, it became clear that Richard was the best basketball player. Bill wasn't bad, but he wasn't as consistent as Richard. Richard made every shot but one, while Bill missed as many as he made. Striker and Charlie definitely were the worst; they missed the majority of their shots and, sometimes, even the backboard.

"Dang," said Charlie, after he missed a free throw.

"That's all right," said Richard. "We'll make it up on the other challenges."

"We'll have to," said Striker as he watched the other teams practicing. "Those other teams all look like they're better than us at basketball."

And indeed, the other teams were making more of their shots than Striker's team had.

"That's okay," said Bill. "We'll surprise them. Let's go try the tire run."

Dropping their basketball back on the court, the boys ran to one of the tire runs laid out on the ground. They practiced running through the tires as quickly as they could, lifting their knees high so that they wouldn't trip.

Charlie excelled at the tires. He was very light on his feet and moved easily through the tire run while the other boys had to go more slowly to keep from falling over. On one practice run, Richard even tripped at the very last tire and hit the dirt with a loud thud.

On the whole, they were better than they had been at basketball, but they were still far from the fastest team.

"Geez," said Bill, watching the team on the other tire run. "Look at them go!"

That team had four members who all managed to get through the tires pretty quickly. At least no one looks like they are about to fall over, thought Striker.

"We'll just have to count on Charlie here to pull us through," said Richard, throwing an arm over Charlie's shoulder. "Come on, let's go run those bases."

Finally, a challenge where Striker felt he could contribute. He was the first to finish the entire lap, with Bill following a close second. He and Bill were so much faster that Richard and Charlie had not even rounded third by the time they each tagged home plate.

The four boys collapsed on the grass to catch their breath. They watched the other teams practicing on the baseball field.

"Is it just me," said Richard, propping himself up on his elbows, "or are we the underdogs here?"

It still seemed that they wouldn't be fast enough to win the race. The other teams weren't as quick as Striker and Bill, but most didn't have any particularly poky teammates slowing them down either. Taken as a whole, they were probably faster than Striker's team.

Charlie nodded glumly while Bill said, "We're just too uneven. The other teams are better all-around than we are."

"So much for winning," said Richard.

"Maybe not," said Striker. "I've got an idea, as long as we can hang back and be the last team to compete." He jumped up. "Come on. Let's go practice the rope swing. I'll tell you all the plan on the way over."

* * *

Ten minutes later, the races began. Each team was timed. Striker's team won by a landslide.

How did they do it?

Solution

Striker's team was composed of four boys with very different talents. While Striker and Bill were both very fast runners, neither was very good at basketball or the tires. Richard was great at basketball, but not at anything else. Charlie nailed the tire run, but that was about it.

If all four members had to participate in each activity, the average of the group would be fairly low. But then, Striker had a great idea. They would specialize.

To specialize means to focus on what you do best. If you're a wonderful piano player, you might specialize in the piano and not spend time practicing the violin or flute. If you're a talented artist, you'll probably spend more time painting than you will, say, building things. By specializing, you can focus on what you're best at.

When everyone focuses on what they're best at, the overall achievements of a group can increase. People spend less time doing tasks they're not good at, and let someone else handle it instead. Great cooks let great writers write books, while those same cooks get better and better at creating delicious recipes. And the cool thing is that, after specialization, we end up with better books and tastier food than if the writers and cooks had each tried to both write and cook.

Striker thought carefully about the rules that Jamie had given and realized that at no point did Jamie say that each kid had to participate in every single activity. He only said that each team had to complete the required tasks: four laps around the bases, four baskets, four laps through the tires, etc. So Striker suggested that they all do what they do best.

When it came time for the race, Striker ran the first lap around the bases and then tagged off to Bill. Bill finished his lap and then tagged off to Striker again, who then tagged back to Bill.

Then all four team members rushed off to the basketball courts, where Richard easily scored four baskets in a row.

From there, Charlie attacked the tire run. With his light feet, he was able to go back and forth four times through the tires more quickly than even the next fastest team.

Finally, all four boys dashed to the rope swing. Striker swung quickly over the sand and passed the rope back to Bill. Bill sailed the rope to Richard, who swung over and sent the rope back to Charlie.

More quickly than any other team, they were finished!

* * *

After finishing the race, the entire group headed into lunch, with Striker, Bill, Charlie, and Richard leading the way.

They sat down at a table together, each setting down a tray loaded with a sloppy joe, homemade chips, a banana, and a freshly baked brownie.

"Man, Jamie wasn't kidding," said Richard. "I'm starved!" He took a huge bite out of his sandwich.

"Mmmphhee too," said Charlie with a mouth full of banana.

Striker laughed. "So you're actually Ralph's cousin, huh?"

Charlie nodded, finishing off his banana.

"Weird," said Bill. He leaned back in his chair and balanced on the two back legs.

"What's weird?" asked Charlie, wiping his mouth with a napkin.

"It's just that you don't seem anything like him," said Striker.

"What do you mean?"

"Well, how do I put this?" said Bill, plopping his chair back onto the ground. "You're kind of . . . nice. Ralph's kind of . . . not."

"Real delicate, Bill," said Striker.

"Well, it's true!"

Charlie looked discouraged. Here he thought he was being tough all day, and now they were calling him nice! This was harder than he'd thought it would be.

"What's wrong, Charlie?" asked Richard.

Charlie shook himself out of his daze. Time to try again. "Nothing. I was just . . . thinking . . . something rugged. And manly."

"Okay," said Bill slowly. He shrugged at Striker and went back to eating his brownie.

Chapter 4

A Place of Their Own

"Wow, this place is gross." Sheila carefully stepped her way into the camp swim shack, followed by Amy and Striker.

The swim shack housed all the camp swimming supplies: beach towels, beach balls, water volleyball nets, masks, flippers – everything you need to have a great time in the water.

All the campers had free access to the shack and everything in it. Unfortunately, it was also starting to look like it. Beach towels were strewn all over the floor. Goggles were tangled up in the nets. Shovels and buckets were still filled with sand, shells, and the occasional snail. A half-empty juice box lay on its side, oozing purple liquid.

Amy gingerly set the juice box right side up again. "Let's just grab some towels and head out to the lake. I feel like we're going to catch some sort of disease in here!"

Out at the lake, they joined Bill and a tall brown-haired girl who were sitting side by side at the water's edge.

"Hey, guys," said Bill. "This is Ruby."

"Hi, Ruby," said Sheila with a smile. "I'm sorry, we don't have an extra towel for you."

"That's okay," said Ruby. "I'll go get one."

"No, no," said Bill, jumping up. "I'll be happy to get one." He turned to Striker. "She can have mine."

Striker handed Ruby the extra towel as Bill sprinted back to the swim shack.

Striker raised his eyebrows at Sheila and Amy, who both looked as though they were trying not to laugh.

"Thanks," said Ruby. "Let's get in. It's hot today!"

After a couple of minutes of splashing and dunking underwater, Striker saw Bill return.

"I ran into Jamie in the swim shack," said Bill, wading out into the water. He dipped his head underwater and came up spitting water out of his mouth.

"He didn't look too happy," he continued.

"Why?" asked Amy.

"Something about how messy it is in there."

"I'm not surprised," said Sheila.

"I just hope we don't have to spend time cleaning it up," said Ruby. "I want to start a club, and that's already taking most of my free time."

"What kind of club?" asked Amy.

"A painting club. Jamie already told me I could use the camp's art supplies. I've just got to find some members and a good place for us to meet."

Sheila looked interested.

"I'd love to join!" said Bill.

Everyone turned to stare at him.

"You like to paint?" asked Striker. "Since when?"

"Come on, Striker," said Bill, lightly punching Striker's arm. "Don't kid around. You know I've always wanted to be a painter."

This time Sheila and Amy couldn't hold in the giggles, but Striker thought they hid them fairly well as they immediately swam towards the floating platform in the center of the lake.

Striker looked at Bill. Bill grinned at Ruby. Ruby squinted at the sun.

"I think I'd better get some more sunscreen," she said and headed for shore.

* * *

That evening at dinner, Jamie made an announcement. "Okay, folks, we've got some housecleaning to do."

They all looked up from their conversations.

"I don't know how many of you have been in the swim shack recently, but it is an absolute mess. You know I love you guys, but I also expect you to take better care of camp property.

"So starting today, campers will take turns cleaning the swim shack. I've posted a chore schedule on the bulletin board that shows when each of you is assigned to duty. Let's see if we can't do a better job."

Amy sighed over her mac and cheese. "I guess we knew it was coming."

* * *

One week later, Striker ventured inside the swim shack to get a kayak paddle. He wasn't sure what to expect after a week's worth of cleaning by the campers.

Looking around, he thought that the swim shack looked a little cleaner, but it wasn't an amazing change. He'd taken his own turn on the cleanup crew a couple of nights before, and it wasn't a terribly exciting job. His group had performed the basics – refolded the beach towels, emptied the buckets, thrown away trash – but whoever had cleaned the shack the previous night didn't even do that.

"Ah, you kids," said a voice behind him. The camp owner Mr. Cutchins entered the room just behind Striker. He surveyed the controlled chaos. "I'd hoped the cleanup rotation would work. After all, it's only one night every couple of weeks. That's not so bad, is it?" He looked at Striker. "I suppose I'll have to come up with a better idea, hmm?" He smiled.

"Actually," said Striker, encouraged by Mr. Cutchins's smile. "I have an idea for you. If you really want the swim shack to be nice and clean, you should let the painting club meet in here."

Why?

Solution

When everyone shares something, people have a tendency to take advantage of it.

With everyone sharing the swim shack, no one took the time to clean up after himself. After all, each kid was just one person among many who were using the shack. Even if someone took the time to clean up after himself, there was no way to guarantee that everyone else would, too. So, it would still be messy. Why bother cleaning up? It was a never-ending – and very messy – cycle.

The best way to break this cycle was to give someone ownership over the shared resource. When someone owns something, he takes better care of it. You take care of your bike or skates, for instance, because they belong to you. No one else can come along and use them without asking you, so you can control whether or not they stay in good condition.

Striker knew that the camp staff needed to give campers a sense of ownership of the swim shack. And he also knew of a small group that was looking for a place of its very own: the painting club.

* * *

Later that week, Striker and Bill went back into the swim shack to borrow masks and fins. Striker almost didn't recognize the room.

The clutter had disappeared. Items were stored neatly in labeled bins, and the beach towels were easily found, folded and stacked on a countertop. The floors were clean, though, if Striker looked very hard, he could find a couple specks of paint that hadn't been there before.

"Wow! It looks great in here," said Bill.

"Yeah, it does," said Striker. "Good job."

"What do you mean, 'good job'?"

"Didn't you help clean it up? You're in the painting club, right?"

"Oh that." Bill waved his hand. "I gave that up after one meeting."

"That fast, huh?"

"Yeah. There was something I'd forgotten."

"What's that?"

"I really hate art."

Striker laughed. "And what about Ruby?"

"I gave her up, too. She said my painting of our cabin looked like a sick moose.

"Of course," he added, "it did look like a sick moose. But there was no reason to tell me so."

Chapter 5

The Midnight Archer

"Something very weird happened last night," announced Richard at breakfast.

"At the bonfire?" asked Striker, referring to the camp's nightly tradition. After Striker and Bill introduced Richard and Charlie to Amy and Sheila, cooking s'mores at the evening bonfire became a ritual for their little group.

Richard slid into a seat between Sheila and Bill at the dining table. "No. After."

"What?" asked Sheila.

"Someone shot an arrow into one of the cabin doors!"

"What? Like into the cabin? Was anyone hurt?" Striker said.

"No, no one was hurt. The arrow literally went into the door. Some guys found it sticking out from the wood this morning when they left for breakfast."

"Wow," said Bill. "Sounds like someone's got it in for them."

"Yeah," said Richard. "I bet they'd give a lot to know who, too."

"Oh, come on," said Sheila. "No one's got it in for anybody." She paused. "And if they did, I don't think they'd take someone out with arrows. We're not living in *Robin Hood*." She giggled.

"Easy for you to say," said Richard. "No one shot at you."

"No one shot at them, either," she said. "Just their door."

* * *

Two nights later, it happened again. This time, kids awoke to find an arrow plunged into the hard dirt path in front of the dining hall.

"Maybe it's some sort of warning," Striker heard a boy say as he and Bill walked up behind the group gathered around the arrow. Other kids joined in.

"A warning about what?"

"Tapioca pudding two days in a row?"

"A meal without tater tots?"

"No soda?"

The group wandered off towards the dining hall door, leaving Striker and Bill behind.

Striker cocked his head sideways and looked at the arrow. "It *is* kind of weird."

"I wouldn't worry about it," said Bill. "It's probably just from the ghost of an Indian warrior. No big deal."

Striker smiled. "Yeah, no big. Hey, what's this?" He reached out and pulled a sinewy strand off the end of the arrow. "Thread? Fishing line?" Striker turned to Bill with a serious expression. "Indian warriors didn't use fishing line, Bill. It must be the ghost of a fisherman."

Bill nodded. "Must be. An arrow-shooting ghost fisherman."

"An arrow-shooting ghost fisherman who wants tater tots in the dining hall."

They walked inside laughing and began to load their trays.

"You know, Bill," said Striker, taking a carton of cereal, "whoever is shooting the arrows could get in trouble if they're caught by a counselor."

"Yes, they could," said Bill. He looked at Striker. "Are you suggesting what I think you're suggesting?"

"I just think we should catch them first," said Striker. "For their own good, of course."

"A stakeout!" said Bill. "Tonight?" Striker nodded with a mischievous grin.

"I love it!"

* * *

After breakfast, the boys headed to the lake with Sheila and Amy. Charlie was already by the shore. He waved to the group before suddenly pulling his hand back down, as if he had thought better of it.

"You know," Bill said quietly to Striker, "I like Charlie, but I don't always understand him."

Striker nodded. They walked down and joined Charlie.

Sheila and Amy planned to paddle a canoe together.

"Just let me put on my sunscreen first," said Sheila. She picked up her bottle and tried to squirt some out, only to find that it was empty.

"Darn," she said. "I need to buy some more."

"Here, use mine," said Amy, tossing an orange bottle to Sheila. "Sarah's taking a few girls into town at lunchtime," she continued, naming one of the girls' counselors. "You could go along and buy some more."

"Good idea," said Sheila, rubbing the sunscreen onto her shoulders. "Thanks." She handed the bottle back to Amy, and together they hauled the canoe into the water.

Striker set off in a red one-person kayak. He had a great time tailing the girls and trying to ram their canoe.

"No!" they yelled, laughing.

"Prepare to be boarded!" he shouted in his best pirate voice. "Avast! Shiver me . . . Whoa!"

He succeeded in ramming the canoe, but he only turned over his much lighter kayak in the process. He surfaced from the water as the girls sped away, waving back at him.

"I don't think you're cut out for pirate life," said Bill. He waded out into the water and helped Striker right his kayak.

"I guess not," said Striker, as Charlie joined them.

Charlie helped Striker pull the kayak onto land, but he abruptly stopped when the boat was only halfway out of the water. Charlie let go again of the kayak and even gave it a little push to propel the boat back into the lake.

Striker and Bill looked at each other as Charlie turned from the water to retrieve his towel.

"Don't ask me," said Striker, going after his kayak.

* * *

After lunch, 30 or so kids gathered to go on a nature hike with Jamie, including Striker and Richard.

Striker looked up from tying his hiking boot and froze with his mouth open.

Sheila was striding down to the group with Amy at her side. But that wasn't the surprising part. Sheila had cut all her hair off!

Where Sheila once had long, wavy hair, she now had a very short, very stylish pixy cut.

"Isn't it fabulous?" said Amy when she saw Striker. "I was just telling Sheila that it's the cutest haircut I've ever seen!"

Sheila looked at Striker, who stood up quickly. Over the past year, Striker had managed to learn to talk to Sheila without feeling like he was about to embarrass himself or throw up or pass out. But now he was looking at a new Sheila all over again.

"Urp," he said.

Sheila smiled. "Thank you."

"All right, kids, let's hit the trail," said Jamie. "We'll be out for a while, so does everyone have their water?"

"Yes!"

"Bug spray?"

"Yes!"

"Sunscreen?"

"Oops," said Sheila. "Amy can I borrow some again?"

"Sure," said Amy. "But didn't you get some in town?"

"No," said Sheila. "I needed to, but I didn't have any money left after my haircut. I'll pay you back. I promise."

Striker went through the nature walk in a daze. Twice Richard grabbed his arm to steer him: once to keep him from taking a wrong turn, and once to pull him out of a thicket. By the end of the trail two hours later, however, Striker felt like he might have recovered his senses.

"See you later, Striker," said Sheila with a wave.

"Urp."

Maybe not.

* * *

That night, Striker and Bill donned dark clothing, grabbed their flashlights, and slipped out of their cabins. At Bill's insistence, they smeared a little mud on their faces.

"Gross," said Striker. "Now we smell."

"It'll help us hide," whispered Bill. "Stop complaining, or we'll be too loud to sneak up on anyone." He gestured forward. "Let's go to the game shed. I asked around while you were on the nature hike, and that's where all the archery supplies are kept. Whoever fired the arrows will have to go there first."

"Okay," said Striker.

Together they scurried past the lake, around the dining hall, and to the game shed. They stationed themselves in the bushes just outside the shed door and began to watch.

It was a muggy night, and the air was full of the sounds of frogs and crickets. But slowly, Striker detected another sound – someone was coming!

He elbowed Bill, who nodded back. A dark figure wearing a hoodie and jeans was rushing to the game shed.

"I hope whoever it is doesn't decide to shoot us with an arrow," whispered Bill, tensing to spring.

"Wait," said Striker, grabbing Bill's arm.

"I was just kidding!" said Bill.

"No," said Striker. "I think I know who it is!"

Who is the mystery archer?

Solution

Some items that we buy are needs and some are wants. If it's a need, it's something that we really need to survive. Needs are very important. Obviously, food, water, and shelter are needs, but so are medicine, education, and transportation.

Wants are items that would be nice to have, but that we don't technically need. Some examples of wants are new toys, ballet lessons, or Disney World vacations.

In general, people purchase needs before they purchase wants. In other words, if you only have a limited amount of money, you first buy the things that you need to have. Only if you have money left over do you buy wants, or things that it would be nice to have.

Because he knew the difference between wants and needs, Striker figured out that the mystery archer was . . . Sheila!

When Sheila went to town, it looked like she mixed up her wants and her needs. Striker knew that Sheila really needed sunscreen. Sunscreen is pretty important at summer camp! But instead, she put all her money towards a new haircut, which was seemingly just a want.

If she spent all her money on a want (the haircut) and ignored what she really needed (sunscreen), maybe the haircut was actually more important than it appeared. Maybe the haircut was also a need.

When Striker saw the second arrow in front of the dining hall, it appeared to have a piece of thread or fishing line wrapped around it. But what if that thread was actually hair? Maybe the mystery archer was getting pieces of her hair caught on the arrow!

If that happened to you, a logical step would be to get the hair out of the way – in other words, get a haircut! And that's exactly what Sheila did.

* * *

"I've always wanted to learn how to shoot a bow and arrow," said Sheila. She and the boys were sitting on the floor of the game shed. Her scream when she had stumbled into Bill and Striker in the dark had thankfully loosened up Striker's tongue again.

"My dad used to compete at archery," she continued, "and I thought he'd like it if I tried, too. I was so bad, though, that I've been practicing at night. I didn't want anyone to make fun of me."

"You must have been bad if you shot a cabin," said Bill.

"Yeah, that was an accident," said Sheila. "One of many. I've actually shot a lot of things I wasn't supposed to. Since it was dark, I couldn't always find all the arrows. I guess I missed that one at the cabin."

"And at the dining hall," added Bill.

"Anyways, I'm getting better now, and I think I'm about ready to start practicing in the daylight."

"You'd better," said Striker. "You're going to get in trouble if they catch you."

"Oh, my counselor, Sarah, knows," said Sheila with a laugh. "She gave me permission at first. She wasn't too happy about the arrows I left around camp, though, so she said tonight had to be my last practice."

"Well then," said Striker, standing up, "let's make it a good one!"

* * *

When the archery contest was finally held, Sheila managed third place. She also didn't hit anyone with her arrows.

And if Striker ducked for cover every time she shot an arrow, she never saw.

Chapter 6

Talented or Terrible?

Camp was halfway over, and the campers were all preparing for Parents Day.

Striker was looking forward to showing his parents around. Though he didn't plan to admit it, he missed them. He'd never been away from home for so long before. He couldn't wait to show his mom how he could handle a kayak now, and he was ready to impress his dad by building a fire from scratch.

He shared his plans with Sheila and Amy.

"And don't forget my favorite part of Parents Day," said Sheila. "The talent show!"

"I'm singing in it," said Amy.

"Yeah, I heard about the show," said Striker. "Count me out!"

"You sure you don't want to sing, too?" teased Amy. Amy had given Striker singing lessons for a brief time during the previous school year. They were not successful.

"You don't have to perform," said Sheila. "But it's really fun to watch. In fact, they start rehearsals this afternoon. We should slip in and get a sneak peak." She turned to Amy. "You wouldn't mind, would you?"

"Mind what?" asked Richard, joining them.

"Us watching the talent show rehearsals," said Sheila. "Amy's going to be singing."

"Yeah, let's go!" said Richard. "We can give you moral support."

"I never needed moral support in my life," Amy said, lifting her chin, "but you are welcome to come and watch."

* * *

After lunch, the dining hall was transformed into a makeshift auditorium. There weren't any chairs set up yet, but a section of one side of the room was roped off as the stage. Striker and his friends sat on the gray linoleum floor to watch along with a few other campers who wandered in.

"Will they be able to fit everyone in here for the actual show?" he asked Sheila.

"It's normally a little tight," she said, "but it's not like everybody comes. Usually, it's only the parents who have kids in the show and some of the other campers. There's a parent/kid volleyball game being held outside at the same time. That'll take some of the crowd away."

They watched as the first boy took the stage. He performed some magic tricks and told a few mildly funny jokes. Striker and his friends laughed at all the right parts and applauded at the end.

Next was a group of three girls who performed a hip-hop dance together, followed by a girl who demonstrated some karate moves.

Amy came onto stage next and belted out a blues song. Her strong voice echoed around the dining hall and captured everyone's attention.

"That was really good," said Richard, clapping loudly with the rest of the small audience at the end of the number.

"That's Amy," said Striker with a grin.

"Next up, Sam and Harry Newton," said the counselor organizing the show.

Sam and Harry were twin boys. They were short and wiry with light brown hair.

"I'm Sam." He waved to the audience.

"And I'm Harry."

"Ooh, twins," said Sheila. "I wonder what their act is."

Sam intertwined his fingers to make a step with his hands. "One, two, three," he counted. With a suddenness that was startling, Harry stepped into his brother's hands and flipped backward!

What followed was the coolest display of acrobatics that Striker had ever seen. The boys cartwheeled around each other, flipped one another, and threw each other into the air. At one point, they bounced back and forth on a small seesaw, sending one person up and then the other, until Sam finally turned a double-summersault in midair and landed with his arms outstretched.

At the end of the show, everyone in the audience and even the other performers stood on their feet and cheered.

"Wow!" said Richard over the noise. "That was amazing!"

"I know!" said Striker.

Harry and Sam grinned and bowed together before dashing off the stage.

* * *

That night at dinner, the main topic of conversation was the acrobat routine. Even those who hadn't seen the show were talking about Harry and Sam and making plans to see the act.

"I couldn't believe those two," said Amy, sitting down with her tray at the group's regular table. "How do you even learn to do that?" She shook her head in amazement.

"I think there's going to be a huge crowd at the rehearsal tomorrow," said Sheila.

"There's another rehearsal?" asked Striker.

Sheila nodded. "Yes, just one more before the actual talent show."

"Awesome," said Striker. "I'm looking forward to seeing them perform again."

"Yeah," said Bill. "I want to see what everyone is yapping about!"

* * *

The next day, the rehearsal was packed. So many people attended that it felt like the actual show.

"I don't know how they can possibly fit parents in here, too," said Striker. He and Bill were stationed on the floor ready to watch.

"No kidding," said Bill. "Ouch!" He quickly lifted his hand. "I'm getting stepped on!"

"Oops. Sorry." Bill and Striker looked up. It was Sam from the acrobatics act.

"Hi," said Striker. "I watched you and your brother yesterday. You were awesome."

"Thanks." He looked around. "There sure are a lot of people here today."

"Everyone's here to see you guys," said Bill. "I don't think the talent show has ever had such good attendance since I've been coming to camp. The parents are going to have to fight to get in tomorrow."

"Yeah, that's what I was thinking, too," said Sam. "Oh, I see my brother. Gotta run."

"Good luck!" called Striker. He watched Sam join Harry. The two boys looked out at the crowd with concerned expressions on their faces and then began whispering to one another.

I wonder what's up, thought Striker.

The talent show practice began, running in the same order. With all the people, the room was buzzing with energy, and the acts were even better than the day before.

Finally, it was time for the acrobatics display. Sam and Harry took the stage as the entire room quieted down. No one wanted to miss a moment of the performance.

Sam put his hands out. "One, two, three."

Harry jumped into his hand, but, instead of flipping into the air, fell on his backside.

The audience gasped.

Harry stood up and brushed himself off. They went back into their routine. Only seconds later, however, Sam fell when Harry got a bad grip on his hands and was unable to launch him into the air.

The audience murmured as the act went from bad to worse. By the time Harry and Sam reached the seesaw trick, Striker could hardly bear to look. The audience let out a loud groan as Harry and Sam were unable to get their timing right, and Sam was launched sideways off the seesaw. He just barely managed to land on his feet.

When the routine was finally over, the two boys skipped their bows to the stunned and silent audience and slunk offstage.

Bill turned to Striker. "What was that about?"

"I think I know," said Striker. He stood to slip out of the audience as the next act came on stage, a ballet dancer who looked as thoroughly bewildered as the audience. Her music began, and Striker headed for the door where Harry and Sam had just exited.

He found them perched on a railing just outside the dining hall.

"Hi, guys," he said. "That was pretty brutal."

They looked at him suspiciously.

"Yeah," said Harry. "Well, I guess we can't be at the top of our game every time."

"Maybe not," said Striker. "The thing is, I think we can find a solution to your problem without you throwing the whole act."

"What do you mean by that?" asked Sam.

"You know what I mean," said Striker. "You didn't choke. You two performed badly on purpose."

Why did the boys throw the act?

Solution

Everything in this world is scarce. That means that there isn't enough of any one thing to spread around to all the people who want it. When lots of people really want something, or demand it, it can sometimes be a little hard to get.

Harry and Sam had a great act. It was so entertaining that they drove up the number of people who wanted to see them perform. The rehearsal was packed, and they knew it would only get more crowded once parents were added to the mix during the official Parents Day show. Space in the audience was limited, and lots of campers wanted that space for themselves and their parents.

Harry and Sam were concerned that their own parents might not be able to find a space to watch them or, at the very least, that they wouldn't be able to get very good seats.

So, the brothers came up with a solution. They decided to perform badly in the rehearsal, missing tricks and falling down whenever possible. That way, everyone who watched them would think they weren't very good and wouldn't try to come back and see them with their parents the next day. Then Harry and Sam's parents would easily be able to watch them perform their acrobatics routine from great seats.

They weren't particularly happy about the strategy, both with losing face in front of their friends and with the bruises and sore limbs they received from all the trips and falls. Unfortunately, the boys didn't see any other options.

Luckily for them, Striker did.

* * *

At the end of the rehearsal, a counselor stood in front of the kids and made an announcement.

"In light of the high demand for this show," she said, smiling at Striker, "we've added a second showing for Parents Day. We'll have a morning talent show and then repeat it that evening. We want everyone – and everyone's parents – to be able to see all of our talented performers.

"And speaking of talented performers, I have two boys here who would like a second chance to entertain this great audience."

Harry and Sam walked sheepishly onto the stage.

"Let's give them a welcome!"

The audience clapped politely as the boys began their act, but the polite clapping soon built to wild applause. It never let up, and by the end of the performance, everyone was standing and cheering.

Chapter 7

Arts and Crafty Competition

One morning at breakfast, Jamie stood and spoke above the hubbub of the campers' conversations. "Hey, everybody, listen up."

Striker and his friends quit talking as the room fell quiet. Bill froze with his fork full of eggs halfway to his mouth. Striker rolled his eyes and stifled a laugh.

"We've got a camper who would like to make an announcement." Jamie gestured to the girl standing by his side: Ruby.

"Hi," said Ruby. "I just wanted to let you all know that the painting club is sponsoring an arts and crafts competition. Anyone is welcome to submit, and all kinds of crafts are allowed." She paused and consulted a sheet of paper in her hand. "The competition will be held one week from today, and all designs are due in the swim shack the day before. Mr. Cutchins has agreed to be our judge.

"Um, I think that's everything, but if anyone has any questions, please ask me. Thanks!"

The conversations around the room started up again.

"I might enter something," said Sheila. "I made a really cool beaded bracelet a few days ago that might have a chance to win."

"You should," said Amy.

"I bet there will be a lot of entries," said Richard, "with the amount of time some kids spend doing arts and crafts." He took a bite of grits. "You'd think they came to camp solely to make lanyards! Give me sports any day."

"I'm sure there will be plenty of submissions from the painting club," said Striker. "Bill, are you interested?"

The group laughed.

* * *

The next week, Striker and Amy browsed through the contest entries. The crafts were set up on tables lined along the baseball fields. Each entry had a little blue card in front of it with the name of the contestant.

"Ooh, I like that one," said Amy, pointing out a quilted square. It showed the design of a blue bird on a tree limb. "I wonder how anyone had time to make that at camp."

"Look, there's Sheila's bracelet," said Striker. The bracelet featured blue and purple glass beads arranged in a pattern.

"It looks great!" said Amy. "I hope she gets a prize."

"Me, too."

They passed a drawing of a mysterious castle with a red dragon curled around the top of the tallest tower. Then, they saw some contributions from the painting club: a watercolor of the lake at sunset and an oil painting of an old man in a fedora driving a sports car.

Striker looked ahead and saw a group of campers huddled around one table. There were so many spectators that it was impossible to see the entry. "I wonder what's up there," he said, pointing.

"Let's check it out," said Amy. "It must be good!'

And it was. Sitting on the table were five figurines whittled out of wood. About five inches tall, each was a different animal – a beaver, a lion, a giraffe, a bear, and a raccoon. The wood was smooth and shiny, and the animals all looked very realistic. Striker almost expected them to begin moving at any moment.

"They are adorable!" said Amy. "I just love the giraffe!"

"Who made them?" asked Striker.

Amy read the card, "Carol Fitzgerald. I don't know her."

"Me, either. But she is really talented!"

"Look, here comes the judge." Amy pulled Striker to the side and watched Mr. Cutchins stroll through the exhibits, stopping at each to take a closer look. He occasionally smiled or made notes on the clipboard he carried.

When he came to the figurines, he spent more time examining them than he had any of the other entries.

"I think he likes them," said Striker.

"I don't blame him," said Amy. "Come on, let's go back to the beginning. That's where they'll announce the winners."

Striker and Amy wove back through the entries to the opening tables of the competition. They found Sheila with a crowd underneath a large banner that announced the judging time. She looked nervous.

"I hope Mr. Cutchins finishes soon," she said. "I can't take this waiting!"

"Don't worry," said Striker. "Yours was great!"

Amy nodded enthusiastically, and Sheila smiled weakly.

Several minutes later, Mr. Cutchins returned and spoke to the group of campers.

"We had some wonderful exhibits in the first annual arts and crafts competition. First, a big thanks to the painting club for sponsoring the contest! They set up all the tables and made the cards."

There was some polite clapping.

"Next, I'd like to congratulate all the kids who entered the contest. There are some truly fine pieces of art on those tables, and I wish I could give prizes to each of you. If you entered the competition, please raise your hand."

Mr. Cutchins led the campers in a round of more enthusiastic applause.

"All right," he said, smiling. "Now for what you've been waiting for. The winners!"

"In third place is Terry Smith, for his drawing of 'Dragon Castle.' Come on up, Terry."

The campers applauded as a black-haired boy with a wide smile walked to the front by Mr. Cutchins.

"In second place: Sheila Meyers for her beaded bracelet."

Sheila skipped to the front of the group, a bright grin on her face.

"And finally in first place . . . "

"No need to guess who this will be," whispered Amy.

"Carol Fitzgerald for her animal figurines!"

Amy and Striker applauded loudly with the rest of the group as a short, blond girl went to the front.

"Congratulations, Carol!" said Mr. Cutchins. "I was very impressed by your carvings! Where did you learn to whittle like that?"

"I just picked it up, I guess," said Carol.

"Well, it's an amazing talent. As first place winner, you get to pick your prize first. We've got three treats on offer from the dining hall: a peanut butter brownie, a piece of cheesecake, or a raspberry tart."

"Hmm," said Carol. "I'll take the brownie. Thank you!"

Sheila picked the cheesecake, leaving Terry with the tart. The crowd dispersed, and the contestants all went to claim their artwork.

* * *

That evening, Striker was walking to dinner by himself through the cabins when he heard a strange noise. It almost sounded as though someone were choking.

"Hello?" called Striker.

The sound only continued.

Striker couldn't tell which cabin the noise was coming from.

"Hello?" he repeated. "Do you need help?"

This time the coughing was loud enough for Striker to identify the correct cabin.

He dashed to the door of Cabin 2 and pushed it open. Inside, he saw Charlie sitting on his bed, holding his throat and coughing. His face was slowly turning blue.

"Oh, my gosh!" said Striker. "Charlie! What's wrong?"

Charlie coughed some more and pushed himself off his bed and across the room. He went to his dresser and pulled open the top drawer. He paused and let out several coughs.

Striker ran to his side. "What do you need? Can I help?"

Charlie shook his head and rummaged in his drawer. He threw several pairs of white socks and t-shirts onto the floor as he searched. Finally, he pulled out something that looked like a thick marker.

"EpiPen," read Striker.

Striker watched in fascination as Charlie, even as he continued to cough and hack, flipped the top off to reveal a shot inside. Charlie held it to his leg and pressed a button that sent a needle through his pants and into his skin.

"Whoa!" Striker said in surprise.

Charlie held the shot to his leg for a few seconds before pulling it out and staggering to the bed. He fell backwards onto the patchwork quilt and groaned.

"Charlie," said Striker, slowly walking to the bed. "Are you okay?" He hovered nearby, unsure of what to do.

Charlie groaned and nodded weakly, and Striker was relieved to see the pink returning to Charlie's face. Gradually the coughing eased, and Charlie was able to sit up again.

"Sorry," he said. "Didn't mean to scare you." He cleared his throat and stood up slowly. "I had an allergic reaction."

"Where are you going?" asked Striker. "Shouldn't you sit down a little longer?"

"Can't," said Charlie. "The EpiPen only buys me time. I've got to get to the nurse before the reaction kicks in again."

"Okay," said Striker. "Then I'll help you."

They set out from the cabin, Charlie walking more slowly than normal, but otherwise looking better.

"What did you eat?" asked Striker.

"Something I shouldn't have," said Charlie. "I didn't realize it had peanuts in it."

"Oh," said Striker. "I'm glad you're all right."

"Thanks," said Charlie. "Me, too!"

"Charlie," said Striker after a moment, "you don't whittle, do you?"

How did Striker guess?

Solution

A basic rule of human behavior is that we make better decisions for ourselves than other people can make for us. No one knows our preferences and requirements as well as we do ourselves, and so we're the best people to make our own decisions.

Charlie knew he was allergic to peanuts, and so he would avoid any food that he knew had peanuts in it. But what if he was given a dessert that he didn't realize also included peanut butter?

Carol gave Charlie half of the peanut butter brownie that she won for first prize. But why did she share it with him? Because, in actuality, it was Charlie's prize!

Charlie loved to whittle, and he was very talented. But in his constant quest to remake his image, he didn't want everyone to know about his hobby.

The solution? Carol would enter his figurines in the contest for him. If he won, they would share the prize.

Unfortunately, Carol could not make a decision for Charlie as well as Charlie would have been able to for himself. She unwittingly picked a dessert that Charlie was allergic to, and that made Charlie very sick.

* * *

Striker sat with Charlie on hard plastic chairs while the nurse administered medicine.

"Why'd you hide it?" he asked, after she left the room to retrieve supplies. "Your carvings were awesome. I wish I could do something like that!"

"I don't know," said Charlie. "I started this summer all ready to build a new identity for myself. I got picked on all school year, and I wanted this summer to be different. I'd be the tough guy for once, like my cousin Ralph. I thought if I entered an arts and crafts competition, it wouldn't exactly help build my macho image."

"Wait a minute," said Striker. "You want to be like Ralph? But, Charlie, no one likes him. No one ever likes the bully."

Charlie sighed. "Maybe. But I just wanted to be tough. Too tough for people to tease."

Striker gaped at him. "Charlie, you just stabbed yourself in the leg without even hesitating! I think that's possibly the toughest thing I've ever seen."

Charlie looked at Striker. "Really?"

"Really. Besides, we all like you just as you are now. Who cares about images and junk?"

The nurse came back into the room.

"Okie dokie, you're good to go now. But do me a favor, and no more peanuts! There's no need to prove how tough you are!"

"Just what I was saying," said Striker with a grin.

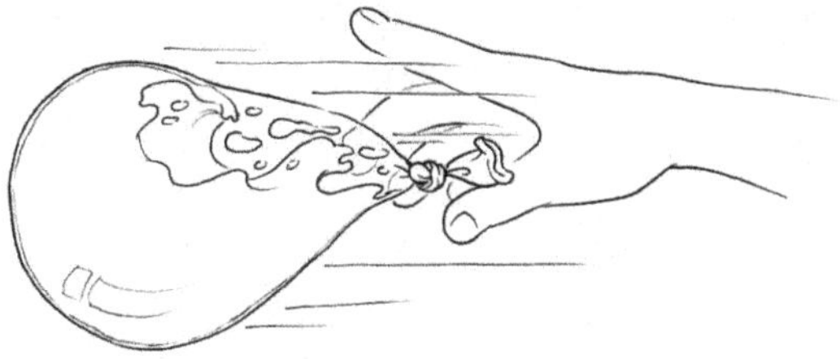

Chapter 8

Water War

After the excitement of Parents Day and the arts and crafts competition, Camp Leopold fell into a quiet period. Calm lasted for a few days until it was broken by war – a water balloon war.

No one knew exactly who fired the first shot. But within days, the campground had turned into ground zero for flying water missiles.

All the kids played a part, dousing each other amid shrieks of laughter. They took to carrying water balloons on them at all times so that they were always armed. They launched sneak attacks, and a group of kids even built a giant water balloon launcher.

Campers never knew when they might stumble into an ambush. It was impossible to walk from the cabins to the sports fields without being fired upon. Kids came into the dining hall for meals soaking wet. No sooner would someone finish drying off from a swim in the lake than he was pelted with balloons.

* * *

One morning before breakfast, Jamie gathered all the campers together outside the dining hall for an announcement.

"Kids, this water balloon war has got to stop!" He held his hands up to quiet the buzzing whispers that broke out around the crowd. "I won't deny that it's been fun, but I'm getting complaints from people caught in the crossfire. Y'all hit three counselors yesterday alone!"

"No!" whispered Amy to Striker. "I love the water balloons! This has been the best week of camp!"

"I know," said Striker. "And I was finally perfecting my signature Balloon Rocket Toss!"

"You can still use the balloons among yourselves," said Jamie.

"Whew," said Striker. "My Rocket Toss won't be wasted!"

"But," Jamie continued, "I don't want to hear about any more ambushes, do you understand? Water balloons are for fun; they don't need to terrorize people who don't want to participate. We've got plenty of other exciting activities here at camp to keep you busy. Now, go eat!"

The kids turned and walked into breakfast.

"Well, that's a bummer," said Bill, as he sat down at their usual table.

"Sorry, what'd you say?" asked Sheila. She was busy hunting down a broken red balloon from her hair.

"I said it's a bummer," said Bill. "Jamie ending the water balloon fight."

"Well, he didn't exactly end the fight," said Sheila. "Just the ambushes. And that's not such a bad thing." She'd located the balloon fragment and was examining it. "I won't miss looking over my shoulder for attacks all day."

"But that's the best part!" said Striker. "The anticipation and the strategy and the . . ." He glanced at Bill and broke off. "Um, you're dripping, Bill." Striker pointed above Bill's eyebrow.

"Oh, thanks," said Bill, wiping away the water. "I got hit on the way over." He grabbed the deflated balloon from Sheila and shot it like a rubber band across the table.

"Ouch!" said Amy.

"Oops, sorry," said Bill. "I guess balloons are weapons even when they're not filled with water."

* * *

That evening Striker and his friends gathered around the nightly bonfire. Amy and Bill were each roasting marshmallows, while Striker and Sheila ate s'mores.

Richard and Charlie watched them longingly.

"Um," said Amy, disconcerted. "Would you two like some s'mores? You need help making them or something?"

Charlie groaned. "No, thanks. We can't."

"Um . . . why?" asked Bill.

"Some of us guys went on a hike today with Sarah," said Richard. He looked around and lowered his voice. "You know," he addressed Bill and Striker, "that really cute counselor with the long black hair?"

They nodded.

"Anyways," he said, straightening up, "while we were hiking, she told us about how she's on this health food kick, and she asked if we wanted to join her for a week or so."

"She talked a lot about nutrition and healthy eating habits," said Charlie, "and all that garbage."

"Charlie!" said Richard.

"I mean, all that . . . information."

"Anyways," said Richard, "she asked those of us on the hike if we wanted to join her in eating healthy as a sort of challenge."

"And Richard made us say yes," Charlie said.

"Why?" asked Bill.

"Let me guess," said Amy with a laugh. "It's because she's 'really cute with long black hair,' right?"

"That's the general idea," said Richard with a grin.

"So now we're not supposed to eat s'mores," said Charlie over the group's laughter, "or any other delicious snack."

Striker looked around the fire and noticed several other campers abstaining from the gooey treats. One kid glumly ate an apple while eyeing his neighbor's marshmallow.

"I'm impressed," said Sheila. "The things you'll do for love." She looked at Charlie. "And for a friend."

"We figure we can make it a week," said Richard, throwing his arm over Charlie's shoulder. "Right, Charlie? Charlie?"

But Charlie was too busy eyeing the chocolate bars on the refreshment table to hear him.

* * *

The water balloon truce lasted for exactly one day. The very next morning, Striker and Bill were walking down the path to breakfast when they heard a stick snap.

Their experience over the past week had trained them well. With one quick look at each other, Striker and Bill jumped behind the nearest bushes and crouched down.

"Someone's hiding up there," said Bill. "It's gotta be an ambush!"

Striker nodded, holding a finger to his lips. He had just heard someone else on the path behind them. He pointed over his shoulder with his thumb.

Bill's eyes widened. "They'll be attacked!" he whispered.

"What should we do?" asked Striker.

Bill hesitated for a moment before jumping up. "Watch out!" he called. But it was too late.

Striker and Bill watched in slow motion as three water balloons flew into the air, splattering onto the unsuspecting traveler's shirt, shoes, and forehead, knocking off his glasses.

When the air cleared, Striker's stomach dropped. The victim wasn't another camper.

It was Mr. Cutchins.

"Oh, boy," whispered Striker.

Mr. Cutchins froze for a moment, staring down at his soaked clothes. He squinted into the trees. Striker could hear the sounds of someone beating a hasty retreat.

"Here you go," said Bill, stepping onto the path and handing Mr. Cutchins his glasses from the ground.

"Thanks," said Mr. Cutchins. He dried his glasses on a corner of his shirt before putting them back on. "I don't suppose either of you saw who threw the balloons, did you?"

The boys shook their heads. "We're sorry," added Striker.

"That's okay," said Mr. Cutchins. He smiled faintly at Bill. "Thanks for trying to warn me."

He turned and headed toward the dining hall, walking stiffly in his wet clothes. Striker and Bill followed a few moments later. As they approached the building, several kids turned their heads to watch a very soggy Mr. Cutchins pass the dining hall and head to the camp office.

* * *

Before lunch that day, Mr. Cutchins called a meeting with all the girls.

"Well, ladies, it seems I got in the way of another water balloon ambush this morning." The girls all looked uncertainly at one another.

"Excuse me, Mr. Cutchins," said a tall brunette raising her hand in the front. "Why are only the girls here?"

"Good question, Miss Clooney. Because although my glasses were knocked off, I could see well enough to tell it was three girls who ambushed me."

"Oh." The girl sunk back into the crowd.

"I'm sorry to see that some of you didn't take Jamie's instructions seriously," Mr. Cutchins said, fixing the group with a stern expression. "Would anyone care to confess to the ambush?"

No one spoke.

"Sure?" asked Mr. Cutchins. Still, he met only silence. "All right," he said with a sigh. "Then I'm afraid I'm going to have to take more severe measures. Unless someone chooses to admit to this morning's ambush, all girls will be banned from using water balloons for the rest of camp."

A stunned silence greeted this announcement.

Mr. Cutchins looked at the girls sympathetically. "I'm sorry, ladies. I hope next time you will all listen. And if anyone wants to 'fess up, you know where to find me."

Mr. Cutchins gestured for the girls to go into the dining hall, where word quickly spread about the punishment.

"That's too bad," said Striker.

"And it's unfair!" said Sheila. "Whoever it is should have just stopped the ambushes when Jamie told them to."

"But how could they?" said Bill. "Water balloons are like an addiction." He sat up straighter while staring into the distance. "Water balloons are power. Such a little missile that can do so much damage. With a water balloon in your hand, you feel like you can take over the world." He stopped abruptly and lowered the fist that he had pumped into the air. He cleared his throat.

Striker stared at him. Finally, he said, "If you hadn't been standing by me when it happened, I'd think it was you who ambushed Mr. Cutchins."

Bill laughed.

"Well, maybe someone will come forward and admit to it," said Charlie, picking up a carrot stick. "Then you girls can rejoin the fight."

"I hope so," said Amy. She crossed her arms on the table and propped her chin on them. She watched Charlie for a moment. "Still eating healthy, I see."

"Unfortunately, yes." He took a bite, crunching loudly in Richard's direction with his mouth open.

Richard laughed. "You can do it, buddy! Have I mentioned that I really appreciate it?"

"No." Charlie took another bite of carrot, an unsettling gleam in his eye.

* * *

Two days later, a group of campers was ambushed on its way to the swim shack. The kids ran whooping and yelling as water balloons hit the path around them. Whoever started the ambush got away, but when questioned by Jamie, the kids claimed they had seen a few girls throwing the balloons.

"Great," said Bill as he and Striker sat down at their lunch table. Sheila, Amy, and Richard were already eating. "Banning balloons for the girls didn't work, so now I bet they ban balloons for all of us."

"No kidding," said Striker, opening his milk and looking around at his friends. "How's the rabbit food?" he asked Richard.

"Eh," Richard said, biting an apple. "I'll be honest. It's not great." He leaned across towards Striker. "Not that I'd say that with Charlie around." He looked across the room where Sarah stood supervising the room. He gave a cheerful wave when she glanced his way and grinned when she waved back. "But it's worth it."

"Sure is," said a deep voice. It belonged to a tall boy a couple years older than them who was passing by their table. The boy paused for a moment to wave at Sarah as well. "But still," he said after his wave was returned, "it's easier with the help of a few extra rations." He winked at Richard and walked away.

Striker looked questioningly at Richard.

"I dunno," he said.

Striker turned and watched the boy sit down at a table. Then his eyes wandered around the room.

First Striker noticed a boy with green eyes and glasses unwrap a piece of candy under the table. He then spied a tall, lanky kid who looked around guiltily before popping a marshmallow into his mouth.

"Looks like that guy dropped something," said Amy, reaching down to the floor. She lifted a napkin. Underneath was a full-sized chocolate bar.

"Guess somebody fell off the healthy wagon," said Bill.

"I think a lot of people did," said Striker. He stood up.

"Where are you going?" asked Bill.

"To stop this all from getting worse."

* * *

Outside the dining hall, Striker saw Sarah speaking to Jamie. "I don't know where they're getting them from," she said. "I'm certainly not handing them out."

"And I'm only giving balloons to the guys, with strict instructions to keep them to themselves," said Jamie. He sighed in exasperation.

"Excuse me," said Striker. "I think I can help."

Jamie and Sarah looked around.

"Hi, Striker," said Jamie. "Are you telling me that you know who is giving the balloons to the girls?"

"Well, I'd rather not say exactly *who*," said Striker, "but I do know how to stop it."

"I'll take it," said Jamie. "How?"

But Striker didn't address himself to Jamie. He turned to Sarah. "Let those poor kids eat s'mores again."

Why?

Solution

Whenever an item is banned, something called a black market usually develops. A black market is the buying and selling of some good outside of the law. It isn't an actual place; it's just people who trade in goods that are controlled in some way.

When the counselors banned girls from using water balloons, the stage was set for a black market to develop.

The girls still wanted balloons, even after they were banned.

Who could get the balloons? The boys. But what could the boys possibly want in return?

When Striker saw some guys sneaking treats at breakfast, he had a pretty good idea of what was going on. There was a trade in banned goods – a black market. Boys who could get water balloons traded with girls who could get them secret sweets. That way, the guys could appear to be following Sarah's healthy eating challenge, without actually giving up the junk food they loved, and the girls would get balloons.

* * *

The next morning, the small group of boys who had given up sweets had their own meeting before breakfast.

Sarah explained that, while she was proud of everyone who had embraced healthy eating, they could all stop the full-scale challenge now.

"Eating healthy is wonderful," she said, "but a few s'mores and other treats can be wonderful, too. Let's find a good balance between the two."

When the guys filed into breakfast a few minutes later, Striker could tell that they were pleased with the talk, but none so much as Charlie. He strode directly to the front of the food line, grabbed a carton of chocolate milk, and chugged it in one long gulp.

* * *

The camp counselors got together and decided there was only one fitting punishment for the water balloon trading.

After lunch that day, all the campers were gathered on the camp soccer field. The sun beat down on them, and Striker wiped sweat from his brow.

"All right," said Jamie. "We're holding one final battle to end all battles. Boys against girls. On each side of the field, you'll find big buckets filled with water balloons for you to use.

"Kids, have a great time and get all of this water balloon mayhem out of your system.

"Counselors . . . "

The campers slowly realized that the counselors – and Mr. Cutchins – had surrounded the group. They were wearing evil grins and holding . . . blasting garden hoses!

"Counselors," shouted Jamie over the squeals, "this is your chance to remind these campers who's boss!"

The carnage began.

Chapter 9

Sabotage at the Starlight Dance

"Is it just me," said Striker at breakfast one morning, "or have all the girls gotten a little . . . giggly?"

Richard and Bill both looked up from their plates of eggs and toast and surveyed the room. Pockets of girls were gathered everywhere. The girls whispered and giggled and snuck looks around at the boys.

"You're right," said Richard. "What's going on?"

"Oh." Bill groaned and hit his hand on his forehead. "I know what it is. I forgot all about it, what with the water balloon war."

"What?" Striker asked. Bill didn't answer right away. "What is it? You look so serious."

Bill sighed. "Bad news, boys. It's almost time for the Starlight Dance."

"Ah," said Richard. "Of course!"

"We have a dance?" asked Striker in alarm. "I didn't know about that!"

"Sorry," said Bill. "I forgot to mention it."

"Oh, man," said Striker.

"What's wrong?" asked Richard. "It'll be fun! Maybe I'll ask Sheila to dance." He wiggled his eyebrows.

"Er, yeah, maybe," Bill said with a quick glance at Striker. "Or Sheila might already plan on dancing with someone else." But Striker looked as though he wasn't even listening. Panic was etched across his features.

Amy and Sheila arrived with their breakfasts. "Morning," said Sheila, putting her plastic tray down beside Striker.

"Hi," Striker said and immediately stood up. "Gotta go." He grabbed his tray and headed for the exit. Halfway out the door, he recollected himself. He came back and put his tray with the dirty dishes. Then he turned again and made a beeline for outside.

Amy and Sheila watched with their mouths open.

"Okay," said Amy. "What was that about?"

"Nothing," said Bill. "He just got some disturbing news. I'm sure he'll snap out of it. Eventually."

* * *

By that afternoon, Striker felt a little better. He and Bill were practicing on the archery range.

"I was being stupid," he said, pulling the bowstring back by his ear. "It's not like Sheila will expect me to ask her to dance." He let the arrow fly, and it hit the edge of the target with a resounding thunk.

"Hey, not bad," he said.

"Whatever you say," said Bill. "But I think you might want to watch out for Richard. He likes Sheila, too. And he didn't turn into a robot with no social skills when I said the word 'dance.'"

"Very funny," said Striker.

Thunk.

"When's the dance?" asked Striker.

"Friday night."

"That's still a few days away. Maybe I'll build up enough courage by then and ask Sheila to dance."

"Or maybe you'll turn into a quivering mass of jelly while Richard sweeps her away."

"Right. Or that."

* * *

Friday evening arrived. The dining hall had been transformed into a ballroom with balloon archways and streamers everywhere. Chairs lined the walls, but the center of the room was clear for dancing. Chinese lanterns hung on one long string, surrounding the room and lighting the floor with bursts of color.

At the front of the hall was a large table set up with fancy stereo equipment, ready to blast music for the campers.

Striker, Bill, Sheila, and Amy stuck their heads into the dining hall to peek at the decorations. Sheila had volunteered along with several other campers to decorate and couldn't wait until the dance began to show off her handiwork.

"Looks good, right?" she said.

"It looks fabulous," said Amy.

"Really nice," agreed Striker.

"Those lanterns are cool," said Bill. "They're going to look awesome once it's dark."

"Thanks, guys," said Sheila. "Quite a few of us worked on it. I think it was worth it."

"Let's go eat," said Amy. There was a camp cookout that evening because the dining hall was set up for the dance. After dinner, the campers would go back to their cabins to change for the party.

* * *

Striker nervously straightened his polo shirt. He knew most of the girls would be wearing dresses, and some of the boys even had on button-down shirts or ties. Since he hadn't known about the dance, however, he only brought a polo and khakis. On the whole, he thought, he was glad about that.

"I'm already freaking out. Why be uncomfortable, too?" he muttered.

Striker walked to the dining hall with a pack of boys, including Richard, Jared, and Chris.

He didn't know what had happened to Bill. They'd eaten together at the cookout and then gone back to the cabins together.

Bill had just changed into a tie when he'd realized that he left his baseball cap at the cookout.

"I'll be right back," he'd said before dashing out the door. But he never returned.

Striker figured he must have gone on to the dance without him.

And I'll get him for that later, too, he thought. He could have used some moral support just then.

He and the boys walked along. Jared and Richard told jokes, while everyone laughed loudly and a little nervously.

They got to the dining hall and walked inside. A group of girls was already there, clustered together in their fancy dresses.

There was no sign of Bill, but Striker saw Sheila right away. She wore a dark blue dress and looked very pretty. But she didn't look happy.

Striker immediately walked to her side. "What's the matter?"

"We've been sabotaged!" she said, pointing around the room. Striker then noticed that the decorations were hanging off the walls. The balloons had floated away; the streamers hung in tatters. And every Chinese lantern had disappeared.

Striker looked around the room quickly. "Are there any clues? Why would anyone do this?"

"I don't know!" said Sheila. "After all our hard work!" She was almost in tears.

Striker walked around the room. He tried to be helpful, but, in truth, he didn't know what he was looking for. He glanced out one of the back windows as he walked by, but then froze. He leaned toward the glass for a better look.

"Sheila!" he called. "Come here!"

Sheila hurried over.

"Look out on the lake," he said. "What do you see?"

"What is – are those the Chinese lanterns?"

Out on the lake floated red, blue, green, and yellow lights.

Sheila peered more closely. "What's that they're holding?" she asked.

"Sheila," said Striker slowly. "I don't think you've been sabotaged. Not exactly. I think the decorations were . . . repurposed."

Striker and Sheila hurried outside, followed closely by the other campers. They dashed to the water's edge and squinted to see what exactly the lanterns were doing in the middle of the lake.

When Striker's eyes adjusted to the darkness, he laughed out loud. Bill was waving to him from a floating island of canoes, all strung together with colorful lanterns.

What do you think happened?

Solution

Resources go to their most productive uses. In other words, we use items where we will get the most good out of them. We might be able to use a surgeon to walk our dog, but we get more use out of her if she spends her time performing surgery. We might be able to use a car to hold up flowerpots, but it is much more useful to drive people around in.

The Chinese lanterns looked very pretty as decorations for the dance. But something happened that made them far more useful in another purpose.

When Bill walked back down to the cookout to find his baseball cap, he noticed something – one by one the canoes were floating off into the center of the lake. Somehow the rope that held them together had come undone and sunk under the water!

As quickly as he could, Bill hurried to find a replacement rope. The first thing that came to his mind was the string that connected all the Chinese lanterns. Without stopping to think, he dashed to the dining hall, ripped down the Chinese lanterns (unfortunately knocking down many of the other decorations in the process), and ran back out to the lake. Just in time, he took a running leap and landed in the last canoe that was floating away.

Out in the water, he used the string, with the lanterns still attached, to connect all the canoes together again. Only after he had created a giant floating island did he realize that he was stranded in the middle of the lake!

* * *

Several of the counselors donned bathing suits and struck out into the water to tow the canoes back to shore.

"Why didn't you just swim back?" asked Striker, laughing after Bill clambered back onto land.

Bill looked shocked. "I'm wearing a tie! My mom would have killed me!"

Everyone laughed.

"You know," said Sheila, "the lanterns do look pretty cool out here."

"Hey!" someone shouted. "Let's move the party to the canoes!"

The crowd of campers roared its approval.

Quickly, the campers relocated the music equipment to an outdoor outlet. Someone retrieved the escaped balloons from the dining hall ceiling and tied them to the edges of the canoes. Everyone piled into the boats carrying punch and treats. They sat back and listened to the music.

"Now this is a true Starlight Dance," said Jamie, surveying the campers bobbing on the water. The stars shone down on the scene.

Somehow, Striker found himself sharing a canoe bench with Sheila. They smiled shyly at each other before looking up at the night sky.

I can handle this, thought Striker. No need to panic. Sheila - good. Music - good. No dancing - good. I'm totally in control.

Without looking at him, Sheila slipped her hand into his.

Urp.

Chapter 10

Goodbyes

"Cannonball!" Striker threw himself off the floating dive platform and splashed into the lake.

"I can do better than that!" yelled Bill. "Geronimo!" He tucked his legs under him and created an enormous splash.

"Oh, please!" said Sheila. "Let's show them, Amy!"

"One, two, three," counted Amy, and the two girls launched themselves off the platform together, creating the biggest splash of all.

It was the sixth and final week of camp, and all the campers were relishing their last days away from home. Everywhere, kids relaxed in the sun, playing games, swimming, or walking with their friends.

Out in the water, Striker and his friends laughed and splashed back and forth. Amy dunked Bill, as Sheila struggled to float on her back.

"Hey, guys," a voice said.

"Whoa!" said Bill, as Charlie's head unexpectedly surfaced right next to him in the water.

"Hey, Charlie," said Amy, treading water. "What's up?"

"You can't guess what I just heard." He gestured for them to follow him back up to the dive platform.

When all of them had hauled themselves out of the water and stretched themselves out in the sun, Charlie broke the news. "Jamie is leaving."

The kids gasped.

"Not Jamie!" said Bill. "How do you know?"

"I just overheard him talking with Mr. Cutchins. They said it was time for them to break up the 'dynamic duo.' And Mr. Cutchins said that he would miss Jamie next year, but that, after the water balloon incident, he thought it was for the best."

"Oh, no," said Sheila. "And it sounds like it's our fault, too! Mr. Cutchins must be mad about getting hit with the water balloons."

"Jamie did tell everyone to stop," said Charlie.

"But they didn't listen," said Amy.

"Geez, I feel terrible," said Bill. "Jamie's the best counselor! He's a big reason why I like to come every year."

"You know," said Amy, "we should do something nice for him. Maybe we could throw him a going-away party."

"Yeah, good idea!" said Bill. "We could surprise him at the bonfire tonight."

"I'm sure the dining hall would let us have some cookies and drinks," said Sheila.

"And we could ask Jared and Chris to play some music," added Charlie.

They all nodded enthusiastically.

"Well, what are we waiting for?" asked Bill. "Let's go spread the word!"

They all jumped off the platform and swam to shore.

* * *

After lunch, Striker, Bill, Charlie, and Richard walked along the lake back towards the cabins, eating rainbow snow cones. The sweltering heat melted the colorful ice quickly. Liquid lines of blue, red, and orange dripped down their hands; the boys licked the cones faster.

Plans for the party were going well. Everyone they talked to was disappointed to hear about Jamie's departure, but they all threw themselves into the party planning. The painting club made a big banner for the party, and some of the girls wrote a tribute to sing to Jamie while Chris and Jared played along. Sheila and Amy even talked the dining hall staff into making enough cupcakes for all the campers and counselors.

"I think we're in pretty good shape," said Bill.

"Hey, look," said Richard. He pointed to the water's edge. "It's Jamie."

"Let's go talk to him," said Striker. "But no one let on that we know he's leaving. We want tonight to be a surprise."

Jamie was in the middle of a building project. He was surrounded by boards and nails and had a toolbox open at his feet.

"Hi, guys," he said as he saw them approach.

"Hey, Jamie," they replied.

"What are you doing?" asked Charlie.

"I'm rebuilding the lifeguard stand," said Jamie. "It's getting rickety and unsafe. We can't have our lifeguard falling over, can we?" He grinned. "Then who would watch all you fellas out in the water?"

The boys were silent for a moment.

"That is just so nice of you," Charlie finally said. The other boys all nodded.

"Well, thanks," said Jamie, laughing. He then paused and shaded his eyes with his hands as he squinted at them.

"Hey, what's wrong with you guys? You look like your dog died!" He paused. "Nobody's dog died, did it?"

"No," said Bill, as the other boys shook their heads and looked sympathetically at Jamie.

"Well, that's good," said Jamie, turning back to his project. "So why the long faces?"

"It's nothing," said Striker. "We were just thinking it's a pretty hot day to be working, that's all."

"Yep, you're right about that." Jamie wiped his forehead. "But you've gotta do what needs doing."

He cheerfully reinforced the joint between two planks with a screw gun.

"I guess," said Charlie.

"Good thing you're being paid," said Richard with a weak laugh.

Jamie smiled. "Actually, I'm not being paid right now. It's my afternoon off."

"It is?" said Bill. "Then, why are you working?"

"If I fix this now, it will save me a lot of effort in the future," said Jamie. "And it will make a nicer – not to mention safer – camp for you kids."

He leaned back to check the newly built frame with a level.

"Looks good," he said, squinting at the level. He turned to the boys. "Now, I want you guys to go have some fun. I'll take care of the work."

"Okay," said Charlie.

"Thanks," added Bill.

They walked away, thoughtfully slurping their snow cones.

"He's pretty awesome," said Richard.

Striker nodded. "He is. But you know . . . I think that we might want to change tonight's party."

"Huh?" asked the boys.

"Don't you think he deserves it?" asked Charlie.

"Of course," said Striker. "But I don't think it should be a going-away party."

What kind of party should it be?

Solution

Jamie isn't the one who is leaving Camp Leopold – Mr. Cutchins is.

When Charlie overhead Mr. Cutchins and Jamie's conversation, he incorrectly assumed that because Mr. Cutchins would miss Jamie the next year, that Jamie was the one leaving.

In truth, Mr. Cutchins was ready to retire. Being attacked in a full-scale water balloon ambush made him realize that he felt too old and too tired to run the summer camp full time. He was ready to hand over the reins. And who best to take over the camp from him but the other half of the "dynamic duo" – everyone's favorite counselor, Jamie?

But how did Striker figure this out?

When the boys found Jamie rebuilding the lifeguard tower, they actually found Jamie investing in the camp.

To invest is to spend money, time, and effort now to raise the standard of living in the future. Jamie saved himself trouble in the future by fixing the lifeguard stand today, before someone got hurt. This was so important to Jamie that he even worked on it on his afternoon off!

If Jamie was leaving the camp, why would he be concerned with saving himself work in the future – he wouldn't be there to enjoy the fruits of his labor!

From that clue, Striker guessed that Jamie would be remaining at camp. But the conversation that Charlie overheard indicated that someone was leaving Camp Leopold. If it wasn't Jamie, then it had to be Mr. Cutchins.

* * *

The party that night around the bonfire was a wonderful celebration. Two banners hung across the picnic tables. One read, "Happy Retirement, Mr. Cutchins!" The other, "Congratulations, Jamie – New Camp Leader!"

Striker loaded his plate with two vanilla cupcakes and sat on a log beside Bill. He leaned back and looked across the fire at the two guests of honor.

Mr. Cutchins and Jamie each wore silly hats that the campers made for them. Jamie pretended to conduct Jared and Chris in the band, while Mr. Cutchins happily munched on a cupcake.

"I wonder what camp will be like with Jamie in charge," said Bill, watching the other campers talking and laughing. Charlie and Richard were hanging out in the middle of a large group of kids. Charlie was trying to tell a story, while Richard kept interrupting to add details. Everyone was laughing.

"I guess we'll just have to come back next year to find out!" said a soft voice behind them.

Striker looked over his shoulder to see Sheila. She and Amy had walked up behind Striker and Bill and were smiling down at them.

Striker grinned and turned back to the fire. "Bring it on."

ABOUT THE AUTHOR

Maggie M. Larche thinks economics is more fun than jumping on a trampoline while eating cotton candy. A Florida native, she currently lives in Daphne, Alabama, with her husband, son, and daughter. Striker Jones was born from her personal fondness for a good mystery.

CPSIA information can be obtained
at www.ICGtesting.com
Printed in the USA
LVHW051613220621
690864LV00012B/1325

9 781484 016909